THE MUPPETS

Little, Brown and Company

Hachette Book Group
237 Park Avenue, New York, NY 10017
Visit our website at www.lb-kids.com

Little, Brown and Company is a division of Hachette Book Group, Inc.
The Little, Brown name and logo are trademarks of Hachette Book Group, Inc.

The publisher is not responsible for websites (or their content) that are not owned by the publisher.

First Edition: April 2012

ISBN: 978-0-316-20134-6

10 9 8 7 6 5 4 3 2 1

IM

Printed in China

Book design by Maria Mercado

THE MUPPETS

Green and Bear It

by Martha T. Ottersley
illustrated by Amy Mebberson

LB

LITTLE, BROWN AND COMPANY
Boston   New York

It was springtime, and the Muppets were putting on a huge show called the Spring Showcase.

Fozzie went to the Muppet Theater to practice his comedy act.

"What's black and white and green all over?" asked Fozzie. "A frog reading a newspaper! Wocka! Wocka!"

Fozzie heard nothing but crickets.

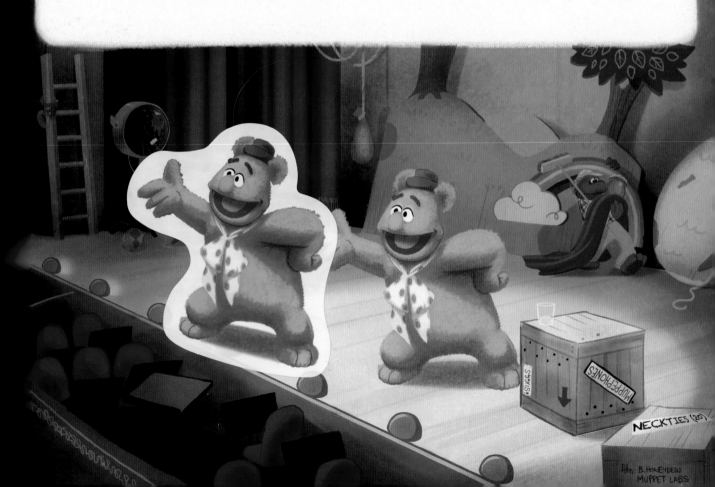

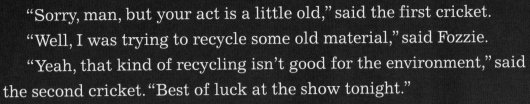

"Sorry, man, but your act is a little old," said the first cricket.

"Well, I was trying to recycle some old material," said Fozzie.

"Yeah, that kind of recycling isn't good for the environment," said the second cricket. "Best of luck at the show tonight."

That's it, thought Fozzie Bear. *I need luck!*

Luckily, Fozzie knew just where to get some.

"Um, excuse me, Bean Bunny," said Fozzie. "I heard a rabbit's foot was lucky, and I really need some luck for my act tonight. Would you mind helping me out?"

"I would like to," said Bean Bunny, "but I'm in charge of finding lunch for my whole family. They are visiting from Boca. Since there are dozens of bunnies to feed, it could take me all afternoon. This meadow in the city park just isn't as green as it used to be."

"Good luck," said Fozzie.

"Thanks," said Bean, and he hightailed it out of there.

Fozzie thought of something else that brings good luck—a horseshoe!

"Excuse me, Mr. Horse," said Fozzie. "I heard a horseshoe is lucky, and I need some luck with my act tonight."

The horse whinnied at Fozzie. "You *do* need help with your act," he said, "but I wear high-tops. I never understood the appeal of horseshoes."

"I understand," said Fozzie. "Sort of."

"Good luck with your act," said Mr. Horse. "I am off to soccer practice. You know, the field in the city park where we play just isn't what it used to be." The horse hoofed it over to the park.

"I need a new plan!" said Fozzie. "I'll just sit in this clover patch in the city park and try to think of one. . . . Wait, I know! Maybe there's a lucky penny somewhere in this clover patch!"

Fozzie started looking for a lucky penny.

After a while, Gonzo and Camilla walked by on their way to the theater.

"Hello, Fozzie," said Gonzo.

"Oh, hi!" said Fozzie. "Don't mind me. I'm just looking for a lucky penny in this clover patch."

"Bawk-aw, bawk-bawk-bawk, bawk-kaw! Bawk-kaw! BAWK-BAWK!" bawked Camilla.

"Camilla is right," said Gonzo. "You should be looking for a lucky four-leaf clover in this clover patch!"

"That's genius!" said Fozzie. "A four-leaf clover is exactly what I need to bring me luck at the show tonight. Thank you, Camilla!"

Fozzie looked and looked. He sniffed. He searched. He scoured. He scanned. He called, "Heeeeeeere, four-leaf clover-clover-clover!"

Nothing.

No four-leaf clovers. Just lots and lots of three-leaf clovers.

Well, if I cannot find *the luck*, thought Fozzie, *maybe I know someone who can* make *it!* The bear ran to see Dr. Bunsen Honeydew at Muppet Labs.

"Greetings, Fozzie," said Bunsen. "My assistant, Beaker, and I were just working on a brand-new cloning machine. So if you see a few hundred Beakers running around, that would be why."

"Beaker must be *beside himself*!" said Fozzie, looking at two Beakers standing next to each other. "Get it?"

The two Beakers shrugged and said, "Meep, meep?"

Fozzie coughed. "Well, uh, I am here on official funny business."

"How can we help?" asked Bunsen.

Fozzie explained that he needed a four-leaf clover in time for the show.

"Not to worry," said Bunsen. "Beaker keeps a four-leaf clover in his diary, the lucky fellow. I think it's why our experiments always turn out so well! We'll just borrow it, and run the clover through the cloning machine."

"MEEP! MEEP! MEEP! MEEP!" yelped different Beakers.

"Don't worry, Beakers," said Bunsen. "What could go wrong?"

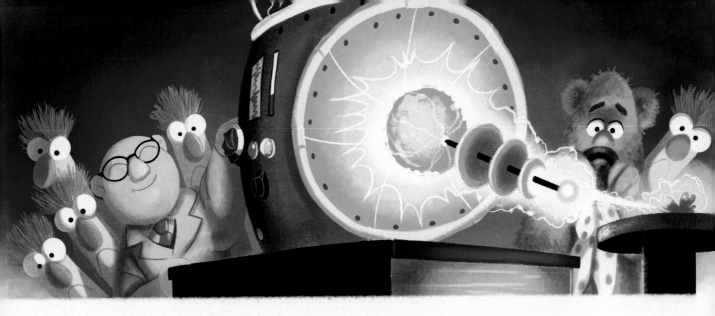

A moment later, Bunsen flipped a switch. The machine's motor purred, the gears clicked, and a tiny puff of green mist shot out.

PLOP! Something fell out into Bunsen's hand.

"Here you are," said Bunsen. "One perfect lucky four-leaf clover."

"Oh, *thank* you," said Fozzie, tucking it into his hat. "This is sure to bring me lots of luck tonight."

A second four-leaf clover shot out of the machine. Then a third. Then a fourth. Then a hundred more!

"MEEEEEEP!" cried the Beakers.

"Oh, dear," said Bunsen. "It seems the cloning machine was set to one squillion."

"One squillion?" asked Fozzie. "How many is that?"

"It is exactly a squillion times more than one," answered Bunsen.

"That sounds like a lot of clover," said Fozzie Bear.

A lot of clover was right! Four-leaf clovers were sprouting EVERYWHERE!

They sprung from the floor, from the walls, and from the ceiling. They grew on every chair, table, and lamp. They grew across the lab, down the street, and on every building.

Fozzie looked at the nearest Beaker. Four-leaf clovers were growing out of his ears!

"MEEEEP!" Beaker yipped.

"Look on the bright side, Beaker," said Bunsen. "Now you are at least eighteen percent more Earth-friendly! Plants clean the air, you know."

Fozzie hurried over to a clover-covered window. He pushed aside the plants and looked out on a clover-covered street, with clover on the sidewalks, the lampposts, and even the cars!

What a clover-covered mess! thought Fozzie. He hurried right over to Kermit the Frog's clover-covered office door.

He stopped and knocked politely.

"Knock, knock," called Fozzie.

"Who's there?" called out Kermit from behind the door.

"Uh . . . Kermit?" asked Fozzie.

"Uh . . . Kermit who?" asked Kermit.

"Uh . . . Kermit please let me in, we have a serious problem!"

"Okay, Fozzie, but I don't get the joke."

Fozzie came in and shut the door. He tried to explain the situation without making it sound too bad. GULP!

"Kermit," he started. "Remember that time when you said it's not easy being green?"

"Sure, Fozzie, I remember," Kermit said.

"Well, first of all, congratulations! You were right. Second, what if there were a whole lot of green four-leaf clovers taking over the city, and it was all my fault, and I didn't know what to do about it, so I came to my best friend, Kermit the Frog, and was really, REALLY sorry? Just a what-if kind of thing . . ."

"Um, Fozzie?" said Kermit. "There's a four-leaf clover growing out of your ear."

"AAAAAAAAAAAAAAAAH!" yelled Fozzie.

"AAAAAAAAAAAAAAAAH!" yelled Kermit.

"AAAAAAAAAAAAAAAAH!" they both yelled.

"I am so sorry, Kermit," said Fozzie. "I just really needed the extra luck for my act tonight. Now, in some ironic plot twist, I've ruined everything."

"Maybe not, Fozzie," said Kermit. "I think I have a plan. We just need to make a few changes to the show. And we need to clear a path to the theater."

Luckily, Fozzie knew some hungry bunnies!

That night, the Muppet Theater was packed for the big show, and the crowd wore green to celebrate. Kermit, of course, was already dressed for the occasion.

"Welcome to a special edition of the Muppet Spring Showcase! Yaaaaaay!" Kermit said. "Tonight's show is extra special, because it's also the first ever Go Green Gala! Our city park just isn't what it used to be, and we think it's time to do something about it.

"Proceeds from tonight's show will be donated to the brand-new Fozzie Bear Lucky Clover Park! The park will have a new soccer field and an all-you-can-eat Bunny Salad Bar, just for starters."

Everyone cheered—especially the Bean Bunny family and Mr. Horse's soccer team.

The curtain rose, and Dr. Teeth and The Electric Mayhem played a rock-and-roll ode to the Earth.

Next, Miss Piggy and several backup chickens performed a "Dance of the Flowers." Miss Piggy wore a sparkling emerald-colored gown. Sweetums served mint milkshakes topped with candied clover.

Finally, it was time for Fozzie to go on.

"Wocka! Wocka!" said Fozzie.

"Wocka! Wocka!" the audience echoed back with huge smiles. That had never happened before! Fozzie smiled.

"Okay, why did the elephant wear his green underwear? Because his *red* underwear was in the wash! Wocka! Wocka!"

The audience roared with laughter. That had never happened before, either.

"Okay, what did the recycled bottle say to the other recycled bottle?" asked Fozzie. "Haven't I seen you around before?"

Again the audience laughed and laughed.

"What do you call a person celebrating Earth Day?" asked Fozzie.

"We don't know. What?" answered the audience.

"A human *green*ing!" yelled Fozzie. The whole audience stood up and cheered. Everyone agreed that it was Fozzie's best show ever—even the crickets.

After the show, one hundred Beakers gave out one hundred clover plants to the audience, so everyone could start their own lucky gardens at home.

Everyone left talking about what a great show it was.

The rest of the cloned clover was replanted in the new Fozzie Bear Lucky Clover Park, just in time for Earth Day.

Later, Kermit and Fozzie lay in a soft field of clover, staring up at the stars.

"That lucky clover really worked," said Fozzie. "Those were the same jokes I told last year. But this time, everyone laughed at them!"

"It might have been the luck," said Kermit, "but everything is funnier when you have a four-leaf clover growing out of your ear!"

Wocka! Wocka!